THE LEGEND OF THE WARE MOOSE

Story *by* Olga Wall

Illustrations by Natalia Logvanova

ISBN: 978-0-578-30024-5
LCCN: 2021921058

Printed in the United States of America

To my children, Sophia, Lauren, and James,
who were born free, in the best country on Earth.

To my parents, who tried their best.
You were right, I would have made a horrible ballerina.

On the western shore of Virginia's Chesapeake Bay, there is a small peninsula known as Ware Neck bound by the North and Ware Rivers. Since Ware Neck is between the Mobjack Bay and the Chesapeake Bay, it is teeming with a variety of land and sea animals, fabulous birds, and interesting plants and trees. Some of its wild residents include majestic bald eagles, cunning red foxes, and even an occasional bobcat!

However, there are certain animals you almost never find in this area. A moose, for example, prefers the colder weather of places like Vermont and Maine. Moose rarely wander so far down south as Virginia.

But according to local legend, there is one such animal that calls Ware Neck its home: the Ware Moose. Locals say that this mysterious creature can sometimes be spotted crossing the North River, from Bohannon to Ware Neck and back, along a path lit by the full moon. No one knows how a moose came to be so far down south, but a full year of luck awaits those who catch a glimpse of the Ware Moose in the moonlight.

On the shores of the North and Ware rivers, which empty direct-
ly into the Chesapeake Bay, a small river otter community has made
its home in the beautiful marshlands of the Ware Neck peninsula. A
young otter named Pip and his mama spend their days there fishing,
crabbing, and relaxing on driftwood with fresh catch in their bellies.

When Pip was just a pup, he was little and silly and would get into trouble if left unattended. So every time Mama Otter went fishing, she took Pip with her. Before she hopped in the water, she would turn to Pip and say, "Baby Pip, I am going out into deep water to get some crabs for dinner. Stay on this beach and wait until I return. If you want to take a swim, stay in the shallow water and do not pass the root of that old tree."

Then Pip's mama would warn him about the sea monster—a mysterious, giant creature with large moss-covered ears who had been seen from time to time in the Ware River.

"Stay on the beach, Baby Pip," Mama would say. "You never know when the creature will decide to visit the river again, nor what kind of appetite it has for an inexperienced little otter like you. I do not want to lose you, little one." Then she would kiss his forehead and swim away.

When Pip was a little older, he grew bored of the shallow water. He wanted to know where his mama went to get all those delicious crabs and fish for their picnics. But every time Pip thought about going beyond the root of the old tree, he remembered his mama's warnings of the sea monster.

As Pip's curiosity overtook his fears, he decided on a plan: he would practice his swimming every day and learn to swim really fast, so if he ever came across the sea monster, he could make his escape without fail.

One day after lunch, Pip's mama told him, "Baby Pip, I am a little tired. I will go take a nap under that driftwood. You stick around and play, and do not go anywhere, okay?"

"Okay," said Pip. But he thought to himself, *This is my chance! I'll let Mama get some rest, and I will go to the deep water and get some fresh fish. When she wakes up, she will thank me and see that I am old enough to go fishing with her!*

Once his mama was asleep, Pip marched confidently down the beach. He saw a bunch of blue herons staring pensively into the water and stopped to greet them.

"Hello, blue herons!" said Pip. "I am going to catch some fish out there in the deep water!"

The blue herons tore their gaze away from the river and looked at Pip in surprise. "Deep water?" one of the herons repeated. "Don't you know about the sea monster, little Pip? You are not safe out there without your mama!"

"Don't worry," said Pip, "I have been practicing swimming really fast, and I think I am pretty good at it now!"

Pip plopped into the water and started swimming. As soon as he reached the deep water, he saw some big brown cownose rays flapping their wings to draw up clams for lunch. They looked at Pip disapprovingly with their wide-set eyes. Pip was scared. *Maybe next time I'll catch a stingray*, he thought to himself. *These rays are way too big for me to catch and carry all the way back.*

Pip swam on until he saw a school of bay anchovies. But he decided not to bother with them either, since they were barely big enough
to be a snack.

Pip felt someone swimming alongside him and turned to see a loggerhead turtle, her large head bobbing in the water.

"How do you do, Mrs. Turtle?" Pip asked, because he was a polite little otter.

"G-o-o-o-d," said the turtle in a long drawl like a trombone. "What are you doing here without your mama, little Pip? Haven't you heard of the moss-eared sea monster who likes to gobble up little mammals?"

"I have," said Pip, nodding rapidly, "but I have been practicing swimming really fast, so I know I can safely swim away if I ever meet him!"

"I do-o-o-o-n't like it," said Mrs. Turtle. "I do-o-o-o-n't like it at all. You should stay near your mama, little Pip. The bay is no place for little otters who have no fear of sea monsters."

"Thank you, Mrs. Turtle," said Pip. "I promise I will be careful."

Pip swam on and on until he could swim no more. He was tired, and his little paws could tread water no longer. *Where can I take some rest?* he thought. *Maybe one of those sandbars on the other side of the river? No, that's too far. Should I swim back? No, I'm too tired. I will never make it.*

Suddenly, Pip saw a driftwood tree strump with its mangled roots moving rhythmically in and out of the water, covered in some kind of moss. The stump was making loud splash noises as it hit the water.

That will do! thought Pip as he climbed on top to take a breath. Just as he was getting comfortable, he felt the tree stump turning beneath him, causing Pip to slide back into the water with a *plop!*

"Hey!" Pip called out. "Tree stump, why are you making such loud noises and moving around for no reason?"

"This is not a tree stump," a deep voice said back. "It is actually my head!"

The deep voice made Pip's heart jump into his throat. *The sea monster!* thought Pip.

Pip was so scared that it took him a second to find his voice. "Who are you?" he said quietly.

"What do you mean 'who'?" the deep voice said. "I am the Ware Moose!"

"Ware Moose?" asked Pip, still barely able to speak from fear. Pip's mind and heart were racing as fast as his little feet were treading water to stay afloat.

The monster slowly lifted his head from the water, and Pip watched with horror and amazement as the longest nose he had ever seen came into his view, followed by a mouth with razor-sharp teeth. Two massive nostrils on either side of the nose slowly opened like giant caves.

Looking way up, Pip saw that what he had thought was a piece of oddly-shaped driftwood was actually a set of fuzzy antlers, with a pair of large pointy ears sticking up between them like antennas.

Pip could hardly contain his fear, and his arms and legs were growing so tired. *I will surely drown, or he will eat me*, worried Pip. But he managed to gather some courage to be brave just a little longer.

He took a deep breath and bowed his head to the Ware Moose. "How do you do, Mr. Moose?" he asked. "My name is Pip. I am very sorry to disturb you. I was just trying to find some fish for my mama, but I got tired and wanted to take a rest on the tree stum—ahh, what looked like a tree stump . . ." Pip ran out of words, and his little legs were giving up from fear and fatigue.

Suddenly, the monster dropped his head down and swooped his right antler under Pip to lift him out of the water. Pip was shaking with fear, but grabbed onto the antlers and held on tight. "Get on top, little one!" the Ware Moose cried, and Pip let go of the antler, slid down its velvety surface, and landed on top of the monster's head.

Pip's heart was still beating hard, but his fear was subsiding. "Are you the sea monster?" he asked quietly.

The moose flicked his ears and let out a laugh. "Sea monster? No, little one! I am not a monster at all!"

"Well then, what are you?" Pip said.

"I am a moose," the giant creature continued. "We moose do not normally live in these parts, but I got lost in my wanderings and I decided to make this my home."

"I am lost too!" said Pip. "So, um . . . you are not going to eat me?"

"No," said the moose. "Don't worry, little one."

Pip's heart finally slowed down, and he blew a sigh of relief. "What were you doing lying under the water?" he asked.

"I am hiding from the heat and the mosquitoes," said the moose. "Those mosquitoes would not leave me alone."

"Why were you making loud splash noises, Uncle Ware Moose?"

"Because I have very big ears, and they splash when I try to swat the mosquitos away."

Pip examined the pointy ears with interest. "Can't you just put your ears into the water?" he asked.

"I cannot put my ears into the water, little one. Water will get inside, and I won't be able to hear well. I live in the deep forest and I need my hearing to be very sharp so I can hear danger."

Pip looked again at the very large ears and the felt-covered antlers. He saw mosquitos attacking the moose's ears and slapped them away with his paws. Then he stroked the big ears tenderly.

"How about your tail, Uncle Ware Moose?" Pip asked. "Could you use your tail to swat mosquitos? My neighbor over on the Ware Neck, a Clydesdale named Maggie, uses her tail to deal with those pesky mosquitoes. Like this." Pip slapped his paws on his sides. "Slap! Slap!"

The moose shook his head, and Pip held on tight to the antlers to keep from swinging off. "The problem, little one," the Ware Moose said, "is that we moose don't have any tails to speak of."

"What?" Pip squeaked. "None at all?"

"Well, we have one, but it is very, very short." The Ware Moose's giant lips lifted into a smile.

Pip jumped off the moose's head and swam around to look at his tail. *Wow!* he thought with pity. *Such a small tail.*

He swam back around to face the Ware Moose. He looked up at the moose's big forehead and bumpy nose. "Uncle Ware Moose," he said, "did you hurt your nose? Why do you have such a large bump on it?"

Ware Moose laughed a deep laugh that rippled the water around him. "No, little one," he said. "This is the kind of bumpy nose that most moose have."

Pip climbed back on top of the moose's head. He thought for a moment, then spoke. "Uncle Ware Moose," Pip said decidedly, "would you like to be my best friend? You could come and share picnics with me and my mama. We always have a lot of fresh fish and crabs. And you will not have to be alone anymore."

"I would love that, little one. I have always wanted to have a best friend, and it *has* been rather lonely without my family. But . . . how do I say it . . . we moose are herbivores, and—"

"Herbi-*what*?" asked Pip with a giggle.

"Herbivores," repeated the Ware Moose. "That means we only eat tree bark, leaves, and twigs and such. And in the summer, we eat the underwater plants, which is what I was doing when you found me. I would love to come and see you, little one," continued the moose, "but the riverbed is full of muddy pits and oyster beds, and I am afraid I will get stuck in the mud and shells."

The moose stood, rising slowly out of the water. Pip held his breath and hung onto the moose's ears while watching the water disappear from his view below. "Wow!" screamed Pip. "You are huge!"

The moose nodded, and Pip slid up and down the felt covered antler bed as if he was on a slide.

"Don't worry," said Pip. "My mama says that during the three days of the full moon, the moonlight will show you a straight, shallow path across the two rivers from the forest to the marsh, which makes it safe for anyone to cross!"

Talking of his mama, Pip suddenly remembered that she would be worried if she woke up and found him gone. "Sorry, Uncle Ware Moose," he said, "but I need to hurry back to my mama, or I'll be in trouble."

"Of course, little one," said the Ware Moose. "I hope you are rested enough to swim back to your mama. Make sure you don't swim this far out again until you are a little stronger."

"Thanks, Uncle Ware Moose," said Pip. He turned to look in the direction of his home and stared across the wide, open water. He thought for a moment. "But . . . but . . . I do not think I can make it all the way back. Do you think you could take me just a little bit closer to my beach? Please, Uncle Ware Moose?"

"Well," said the moose, "you are now my best friend, so I will try. Hang on to my ears, little one!"

The Ware Moose started walking slowly toward Pip's side of the river, putting his hooves into the muddy riverbed one at a time and rocking his body from side to side. Pip sat triumphantly on his head.

As they approached the group of cownose rays Pip had encoun-tered earlier that day, Pip waved at them and smiled, and their wide-set eyes grew even wider with surprise. Then he waved to the blue herons staring at him from the shore, and to the foxes, who had been stalking the herons, but now stopped to watch Pip riding the sea monster.

As they rounded the riverbend, Pip spotted his mama on the shore. She was looking out over the water with her paw cupped over her eyes.

"Look, Mama! Look!" Pip shouted. "I have caught the sea monster!" He stood up tall on the moose's neck and laughed. Then he spoke to the Ware Moose. "Thank you, Uncle Moose! I can make it from here." The Ware Moose stopped and leaned his head down near the water's surface. Pip hopped off the moose's neck and started swimming toward the beach.

"See you when the moon is full, little one!" the moose called after him.

By the time Pip reached the shore, the Ware Moose was gone.

And so, Pip and the Ware Moose became friends.

To this day, the Ware Moose waits till the moon is full to walk along the moonlit path to the Ware Neck shore. There, he waits for the sun to rise, and for Pip to wake up so they can start their days full of adventures.

Stay tuned for the stories of Pip's and Ware Moose's adventures exploring the history and wildlife inhabitants of the Virginia's Chesapeake Bay communities.

About the Author

Olga Wall was born in Moscow, Russia, and grew up in London, England, before immigrating to the United States in 1997. Olga has been working with the United States Agency for International Development for over twenty-five years, providing humanitarian relief and sharing development know-how with global communities in over forty-two countries. Olga loves her adopted country, her adopted state of the Commonwealth of Virginia and, especially, the Ware River on Virginia's Middle Peninsula, where her family owns a riverside property near the historical triangle of Williamsburg, Jamestown, and Yorktown. She shares her love of the area and the Chesapeake Bay wildlife communities with her husband, three children, and two Labradors, Duke and Winston. Her children's sailing camp's lore inspired her to write this story of the Ware Neck critters and the legend of the Ware Moose.

About the Illustrator

Natalia Logvanova, a graduate from the faculty of Fine Arts and Design Basics at the University of Manuilsky in Rivne, Ukraine, currently resides in Nizhny Novgorod, Russia. Having caught the passion for art as a child from her talented father, Natalia specializes in children's literature, having illustrated more than fifty books throughout her twenty-year career. Natalia specializes in watercolor and digital graphics and has brought great joy to children through her vivid illustrations. While most of Natalia's illustrations were published in Russia and South Korea, her art has also been published in England, Jordan, Australia, Poland, Belarus, and the US.

CPSIA information can be obtained
at www.ICGtesting.com
Printed in the USA
BVHW060254061221
621584BV00002B/20

9 780578 300245